For Bryony and Leonie

A Red Fox Book

Published by Random House Children's Books, 61-63 Uxbridge Road, London W5 5SA

A division of Random House UK Ltd

London Melbourne Sydney Auckland Johannesburg and agencies throughout the world

Copyright © David McKee 1994

11 13 15 17 18 16 14 12

First published in Great Britain by Andersen Press Ltd 1994
Red Fox edition 1996

Printed in Singapore

RANDOM HOUSE UK Limited Reg. No. 954009

ISBN 0 09 961061 2

www.kidsatrandomhouse.co.uk

ELMER AND WILBUR

David McKee

RED FOX

Elmer, the patchwork elephant, was
waiting for his cousin, Wilbur, who was
coming to visit him.

"He's late," said Elmer. "Perhaps he's
lost. Let's go and look for him."

"What does Wilbur look like?" asked an elephant.

"Wait and see," chuckled Elmer. "But be careful, Wilbur likes to play tricks, especially with his voice. He's a ventriloquist. He can make his voice sound as if it is coming from a different place to where he is, from anywhere."

"This is fun," said an elephant as they started to search. "It's like hide-and-seek."

Suddenly they heard, "Yo Ho! Elmer! I'm over here."
They rushed to where the voice came from.
"Looking for me?" asked a rather surprised tiger.
"Sorry," said Elmer, "we thought you were my cousin."
"Very funny, Elmer," said the tiger. "Perhaps that's
your cousin I can hear shouting."

"Help!" called the voice. "Help! I've fallen in the pond."

"He has, he has! I can see him!" said an elephant.

"Silly," said Elmer. "That's your own reflection. Keep looking. He's near, but not where his voice is."

They kept looking and all the time they looked,
the voice came from different places. It called,
"COOEEE! Here I am," or "BOO!" to make
them jump. It even came from down a rabbit
hole. The rabbits popped out saying, "That's not
funny. That's not funny at all. That's very silly."

After a lot of searching, an elephant said, "We'll never find him, Elmer. Let's give in."

"Wilbur," called Elmer. "We give in. You can come out now."

"I can't. I'm stuck up a tree," Wilbur's voice said from above them. The elephants giggled. "He's very clever," said one.

"If you don't come," said Elmer, "we'll have to go home without you."

"I really am stuck up a tree," said Wilbur's voice. The elephants giggled again.

"Elmer," said an elephant. "Is Wilbur black and white?"

"Yes. Why?" said Elmer.

"I peeped," said the elephant. "He really is stuck up a tree."

They all looked. There was Wilbur, up a tree.
"Wilbur," gasped Elmer. "How did you get up there?"
"Never mind how I got up, how do I get down?"
said Wilbur.

"I've no idea," said Elmer. "But we're hungry so we're going home for tea. At least we know where you are now. Goodbye, Wilbur. See you tomorrow."

With that Elmer started to lead the other elephants away.
"Oh, Elmer," called Wilbur. "Don't leave me. I'm starving."

"Ha, ha, I was just teasing," laughed Elmer, turning back to Wilbur. "If you walk along the branch it will bend down with your weight and we can help you down."

Wilbur walked slowly along the branch. The branch began to bend down. When the elephants could reach, they pulled the branch the rest of the way and helped Wilbur off.

"Thanks," said Wilbur. "Now, where's that tea you were talking about?" Then laughing and joking together they raced all the way home.

That night, as they lay down to sleep, Elmer said, "Goodnight, Wilbur. Goodnight, Moon." A voice that seemed to come from the moon said, "Goodnight, elephants. Sweet dreams."

Elmer smiled and whispered, "Wilbur, how DID you get up that tree?" But Wilbur was already asleep.

Other Elmer books by David McKee: